LOUIE, the Lonely Lighthouse

Authored by Gregory E. Zschomler

Illustrated by Roxanne Bowman

Layout and book design by Gregory E. Zschomler

ISBN: 1507781857

ISBN-13: 978-1507781852

In Memory of
Lucy Clara Jenkins
U.S. Coast Guard

Dedicated to fellow author
Andy R. Bunch
who encouraged me when I wanted to throw in the towel.

"Let your light so shine before men..." ~*Matthew 5:16*

"It was a dark and stormy night; the rain fell in torrents — except at occasional intervals, when it was checked by a violent gust of wind."* That's exactly the kind of night it was.

Lumiere, or Louie as he is better known, is a lighthouse (one of more than a thousand lining the shores of the United States). He stood as a sentinel against the tempest that churned the ocean waves and blackened the seething skies.

Dark and stormy, indeed.

*The famous line was written by English novelist Edward Bulwer-Lytton as the opening sentence for his 1830 novel *Paul Clifford*.

So murky and tumultuous was the storm that visibility was reduced to less than five-hundred feet. The rain came in sheets. The violent wind blew the deluge sideways. The waves swelled upwards nearing fifty feet in height battering the sharp rocks at Louie's feet, white spray scattering in the gale.

There was a storm hanging inside Louie, too. He was very sad. The gloomy mood washed over him like the seas rolling over the shoreline. He hurt inside.

"I'm so lonely," thought Louie. "No one really loves me."

Louie remembered the previous summer's sunny days, when children played at his base, climbed his stairs, and looked out over the ocean with squeals of delight. He missed the children. He missed the attention. And it seemed that each year there were fewer visitors than the year before.

"Why am I even here?" thought the lighthouse, as the tempest continued to batter his soul.

There were no children. There was no sun. And the heavy weight of winter's gloom hung over Louie like a dark cloud. He'd been reduced to a relic—a historic monument no longer needed for any real purpose.

Modern technology and GPS, or Global Positioning Satellites, had made lighthouses, like himself, all but obsolete. Louie knew what obsolete meant; it meant that he was no longer necessary. He'd been replaced by a world-wide web of technology.

Gone were the days when ships navigated by the sun by day and by the stars at night. Gone were the nights when lighthouses were needed to guide ships safely from hazardous shorelines and into safe harbor. No, Louie was no longer essential. He was only a reminder of things past. Nearly forgotten and, certainly, without a reason to be.

"They might as well tear me down," he thought. "I'm not good for anything important."

The black night of his soul seeped through his being like the rain that made its way into the weathered cracks of Louie's crumbling frame and foundation. Time and nature had taken its toll on the lighthouse, but since he was no longer needed, repairs were no longer a priority and funding was scarce.

The wind and waves continued to torment him, chipping away at his being. He felt the weariness of time and decay wearing down his resolve to continue. Louie sighed mournfully and cast his countenance down in despair. His lonely sigh was answered by a low, woeful echo, barely audible above the crashing surf. But it was no echo. There it was again; unmistakably the desperate wail of a ship in trouble moaning, "Maaaay daaay, maaaay daaay."

"How is a ship in distress?" thought Louie. "They are linked to satellites that guide them."

The deep cry of the ship's horn repeated in the night and Louie felt something rally within him. He knew the ship was alone at sea—and, like himself, wrestling with the wind and waves. He knew he had to act and he had to act quickly, but the despondency he felt held tight to his downcast spirit. He felt so worthless. He didn't matter, so why bother? He was nothing. Nothing. And no one cared.

And still the ship bellowed insistently in the night, requesting aid. And then he saw it in a flash of lightning: a ship dwarfed by the wave it crested before diving helplessly into the deep trough.

"I must try," said the beacon to himself. "Perhaps I am needed after all. In this very hour, maybe I am really all there is."

It took a great deal of resolve for Louie, but he mustered what light remained inside and he cast his gaze out to sea. It had been so long since he seriously needed to illuminate the night. He'd almost forgotten how. But this was his moment to shine.

He didn't feel like it, but shine he did and all the more for it. His faceted beam brightened and cut through the gloom, flashing out over the water, and into the darkness. At the same time, the despair and blackness of his soul began to melt away.

It felt good to do what he was made to do, even if he didn't see a reason for it. It was what he was created to do. And so he willed himself to keep on shining. All through the night he kept his beam sweeping brightly over the water until, at last, the sun crept over the horizon bringing a new day. The storm had passed, too, and Louie could see the ship bobbing, undamaged, on the sea. Louie felt relieved.

"I might have kept that ship from crashing on the rocky shore," thought Louie. But as the ship drifted away along the shore toward the harbor Louie's loneliness returned. Thoughts of doubt crept back and his inner voice began to speak disparagingly to him.

"Don't fool yourself," said the voice inside. "You're crazy if you think you're of any value. That ship had everything it needed without you. You are worthless. You are nothing but an ancient relic."

Despondency again fell upon his soul. As the night wore on, any sense of worth Louie had felt in the night crumbled away, too. His light dimmed and he hung his lantern in despair once more.

At about noon he heard footsteps crunching up the gravel walkway behind him. "What is this?" he thought. "Visitors in the dead of winter?" That was very rare indeed.

"There he is," said a voice he recognized as the Park Ranger. The voice seemed to swell with pride.

"Who?" wondered Louie. "Who are they talking about?"

"Not much to look at these days, but ol' Louie's a strong one," said the ranger.

"Oh," said another voice, "I was looking at him most of the night and, I must say, he was a mighty handsome sight, he was."

Louie, the ranger had said. "They're talking about *me*!" thought the lighthouse, a small spark igniting within him.

"He's a beaut, alright. Needs some repair, but he's still operational. The department doesn't have the funding for anything but the bare bones."

"That's a tragedy," said the man. "He saved our lives last night. We were travelin' blind after that lightning strike wiped out all of our computer navigation and communications systems. I'd hate to see such an important landmark *and life-saver* just crumble away."

"Huh, what?" thought Louie. "Who saved who's life? Me? I saved a life?! I'm...wait a minute, did he call me important?" The fire within Louie burned brighter still.

"Heritage isn't the only reason we keep these torches lit," said the ranger. "Electronic systems can blink out at the drop of a hat. Lighthouses are a reliable back-up system when GPS fails. Yes, there are cheaper automated light towers these days, but some of us like the old ways."

"Well," said the ship's captain, "I'll toast to that! And another thing: You'll have my donation to the restoration fund in the morning. I owe this ol' boy. Many lives and tens of thousands of dollars in crude oil saved last night. Not to mention the cost of clean-up."

Louie felt a gnarled and rough hand pat his side. His pride swelled as the gravel behind him crunched once again as the two voices faded in the distance. The cry of gulls circling overhead and the gentle lap of the ocean brought Louie back to the moment. He stood on the edge of a mighty ocean, at the place where land met water.

The sun beamed through the misty sky causing a great rainbow to arch across the heavens. The sight filled Louie with a surge of joy and hope. Like sunlight mixed with rain created a symbol of hope and promise, his light had brought hope. His light had brought life.

The worthy sentinel stood tall and proud. "I am Louie," he thought. "No! *Lumiere*—the light bearer. I stand in the gap* between life and death."

*Ezekiel 22:30 (The Message Bible): "I looked for someone to stand up for me against all this, to repair the defenses of the city, to take a stand for me and stand in the gap…"

Notes:

Lumiere, pronounced *loo-me-air*, is French for light.

TO THE READER:

It is true that ocean-going vessels mostly navigate electronically these days, but there are still about a thousand lighthouses lining the shores of North America. Most stand along one of our mighty oceans, but there are some that line the shores of inland waters, like the Great Lakes. There are lighthouses still in practical use, but many have fallen on hard times—decommissioned and in some cases demolished.

To find out more about lighthouses and how you can save them visit
http://www.lighthousepreservation.org/ OR *https://uslhs.org/*

In many ways, this tale is autobiographical in that it reflects the soul of a writer in an age where books are being forgotten. Electronic books and, even more so, the internet and gaming, are replacing the love of a good book. (Reading to your child now will assure there are books to be loved in the future.)

There are certainly days I don't feel like writing—days when I question the validity of what I attempt to do for a living. Not every title sells well, and when sales languish, unfortunately, so does the spirit. Writers tend to be tormented souls. Though writing is a solitary experience, stories are meant to be shared with readers. To know one's works are read and enjoyed is a very satisfying feeling.

If you feel like Louie and question your own self-worth there is help available. Please talk to a parent or guidance counselor. Remember, too, that "God don't make junk" and He has a plan for your life.

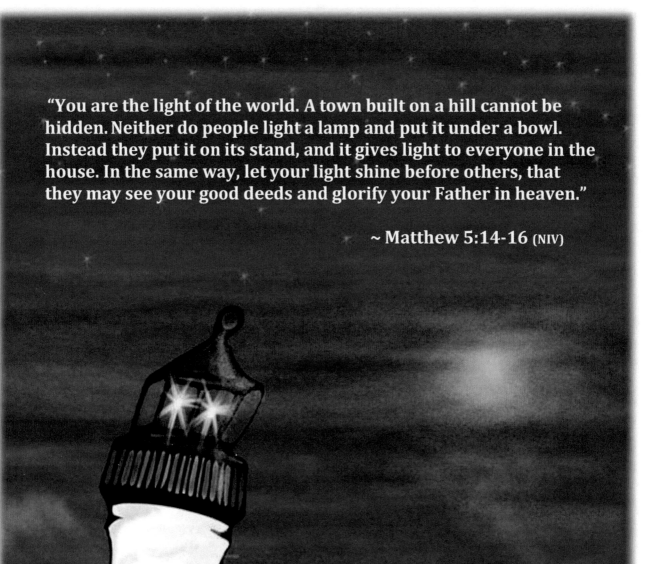

"You are the light of the world. A town built on a hill cannot be hidden. Neither do people light a lamp and put it under a bowl. Instead they put it on its stand, and it gives light to everyone in the house. In the same way, let your light shine before others, that they may see your good deeds and glorify your Father in heaven."

~ Matthew 5:14-16 (NIV)

About the Illustrator

Roxanne Bowman was told at a young age she would amount to nothing. Instead of believing the lie she rallied against it with an attitude of "Watch me suckers!" She was the first person in her family to graduate college and holds an art degree from Stevens-Henager College and, despite dealing with MS, she is a determined and successful artist. Roxanne is a digital artist, painter and graphic designer living at the center of the Oregon coast. She has three daughters, a husband of 33+ years, and three grandchildren. She says that MS took away some of the things she loves, but that God has given back more than she would have ever thought.

About the Author

Gregory E. Zschomler is an author and artist living on Oregon's north coast with his wife of 32 years and two of their eight children. At this point, he's the author of eight other books including three in the **Bayou Boys Adventures** series for middle-readers, the YA novel ***The Amish vs. the Zombies*** (he's working on the screenplay), a book of humor titled ***Rocketman: From the Trailer Park to Insomnia and Beyond***, and another children's picture book ***"I'm Samson," said Sydney*** (illustrated by April M. Bullard). His adventures have taken him to 36 states from coast to coast. He enjoys family, theater, travel, cooking, all things Disney, and time with Jesus. He plans on more books, but no more children (except grandchildren, of which he has three). You can find him on Facebook and Twitter.

Want to see other books by the author?

Scan the QR code with your cellphone or visit:
www.gregoryezschomler.blogspot.com

Made in the USA
Middletown, DE
23 September 2021